# A Pi
# Co~~mmunity~~

## A Short Story of Self Delusion and Pride

Christian Fiction Short Stories: Book 3

by

Natalie Vellacott

Copyright:
Natalie Vellacott 2023
Cover design image: freepik.com
All rights reserved.

# Contents

Chapter 1 ............................................. 4
Chapter 2 ........................................... 14
Chapter 3 ........................................... 19
Chapter 4 ........................................... 26
Chapter 5 ........................................... 32
Chapter 6 ........................................... 43
Chapter 7 ........................................... 51
Chapter 8 ........................................... 58
Chapter 9 ........................................... 62
Chapter 10 ......................................... 68
Chapter 11 ......................................... 75
Chapter 12 ......................................... 84
Chapter 13 ......................................... 87
Chapter 14 ......................................... 93
Chapter 15 ......................................... 98
Note to Reader ................................ 107

# Recap of Books 1 and 2

*In Book 1, <u>I Did It My Way</u>, Annie Yale, a middle aged woman with two teenage children and a turbulent marriage, dies during a routine operation and finds herself at Judgement Day.*

*Her life is reviewed by Jesus and some angels and she sees all of the opportunities she has had to repent and turn to God.*

*During the review, she witnesses her own funeral and her father-in-law, Gary being visibly moved when his grandson, Grant speaks about true faith. However, he quickly shakes it off and follows his wife out of the church.*

*Book 2, <u>The Return</u> is Grant's story as a prodigal wandering from the faith.*

*Book 3, A Pillar of the Community is Gary's story and we join him immediately after the funeral.....*

# Chapter 1

Gary and Janet Yale are sitting in Starbucks drinking coffee. As anticipated, the funeral of their 46 year old daughter in law Annie, had been tough but there had also been an unexpected and disturbing twist. Now, away from the chaos and confusion, they are reflective as they discuss the day's events.

"What did Grant say to you when I went after Dean, you both looked upset?" Janet prompts her husband of 40 years.

"Oh, nothing much. I confronted him about making such a spectacle of himself and asked if it was really the time and place for all that stuff." Gary isn't willing to admit that he had been moved at the funeral so the lie slips easily off his tongue, but he still avoids eye contact with the lady who knows him best.

"That's a bit harsh. I'm sure he was speaking from his heart. He's just become a bit fanatical recently and Annie's funeral gave him a platform. I'm sure he'll regret it when he's had time to grieve properly." Janet assesses her grandson favourably.

"Hmm, maybe. I'm more worried about Dean. Now, what are we going to do about him?" Gary swiftly changes the subject.

"Not much we can do, is there. I mean, he's a grown man. It sounds terrible to say it out loud but I'm not sure that Annie's death will be the worst thing in the world for him. You know they were struggling," Janet voices the concerns they have both had for a while about their son and daughter in law's shaky marriage.

"I don't think that's fair. He wouldn't have wanted her dead," Gary pretends to be shocked by Janet's unusual forthrightness.

"I think he was more wound up by Grant's behaviour. That'll be the difficult issue especially if Grant carries on with his zealous attempts to convert everyone to Christianity. I think you should try and see Dean, or at least give him a call and make sure he's okay later?" Janet waits for her husband to agree to her suggestion.

"Okay, dear," Gary replies dutifully but really he is thinking that Dean just needs to get drunk and then sleep off the hangover.

Later at home,

"Right, I need to go to the church, they don't have anyone to play tonight," Gary says as he heads out of their front door.

"What, couldn't they have given you the night off in light of the funeral?" Janet says, surprised.

"They offered, but I said I didn't mind. You know they rely on me and I like to keep up my skills," Gary grins as he slips out and makes his way to their garage.

He waves at their neighbour but one who is cleaning his car in the driveway.

"Hi, Gary, thought I'd get on and do the car as you've got a lot on at the moment. So sorry to hear about your daughter in law."

"Thanks Albert, but I'm happy to do it. Tell you what, I'll do your lawn tomorrow if you like?" Gary offers.

"Really?" Albert's face lights up. "That'd be great as I've been dreading having to face it, it's these knees that are killing me."

"Of course, no bother," Gary calls back loudly as he opens the garage. Before getting into his car, he takes a quick glance around to see if anyone overhead his generous offer to his elderly neighbour.

He heads for the small parish church just around the corner from their house. It's their mid-week drop in for the homeless. Gary always plays the piano and helps serve the food to the regulars that traipse in and out.

He originally got involved when he gave a few pence to a street beggar who mentioned the church activity. When he had first turned up to offer help, they had suggested he could arrange chairs and tables and do some cleaning. Gary had reluctantly agreed to these mundane tasks although feeling that they were somewhat beneath him as an increasingly important figure in the community, because it meant he could avoid the short God talk that accompanied the men's meal.

However, in time and much to Gary's delight, the church decided to drop the talk completely, believing that their attendees would rather eat in peace. The volunteers could always chat with them one to one if they wanted and get to know them this way rather than preaching at them. The church had since found their numbers sky-rocketing. They had been forced to hire paid staff and to secure regular food donations from local supermarkets. Although some of the "customers" complained about being served the same meals week in and week out and pointed out that their utensils weren't always spotlessly clean, Gary and the church members have been thrilled by the uptake.

Tonight, the church have managed to secure an official photographer from the local paper to give them some publicity in the hope of generating some income. Gary ensures he is visible in the main photo and that he is holding some dirty dishes, demonstrating his willingness to get stuck in.

As soon as the photos have been taken, Gary makes his excuses and leaves the others to deal with the mess. They don't mind as they know he is involved in a lot of local projects and is very busy, they are just grateful that he still spares the time to come and see them each week, even if his visits are getting shorter every time.

Arriving home, Gary parks in his garage then, instead of using the internal door into his kitchen, he heads back around the front in full view of his curtain twitching neighbours. He begins a countdown in his head, "10, 9, 8, 7, 6…."

"Nice evening Mr Yale, where have you been?" Mrs Harma calls as she approaches from across the street.

"Just at the church helping the homeless as usual," Gary smiles smugly.

"Wonderful. If only there were more people like you out there who really cared." Mrs Harma gazes in admiration at her hero neighbour who often cuts her hedge and mows her lawn, only at the front mind you.

"Well, I do my best," Gary flushes slightly despite himself. "I'll do that hedge and lawn for you this week." He ensures he points towards the front.

"Thank you so much, I say, is

there any chance you could do the back some time as well?" Mrs Harma asks.

Gary's been dreading this moment as Mrs Harma has a huge lawn and multiple shrubs and hedges at the back. It would take him weeks to make a dent in it, especially as it's so overgrown.

"I think you'll find that it's better for the wildlife if you leave it as it is," he convincingly replies. "If you cut it all back, they'll stop coming and I know how much you like your daily visitors."

"Oh, do you really think so? I do love to watch them digging and ferreting about, especially the muntjacs and the squirrels. Maybe I should leave it then."

"I'll do the front for you, no problem," Gary hastens back towards his house before she can make any further requests of him. He notices that several of his neighbours are out walking their dogs. He opens his front door and is greeted by his wife.

"How was the meeting?" she smiles. "Cup of tea?"

"Yes, lovely. I just saw Mrs Harma across the street, she was trying to get me to do her back lawns and hedges again. I've reminded her of the wildlife. If you see her, perhaps you can mention how amazing it all is to back me up?"

"You're terrible," Mrs Yale laughs at her husband's deviousness. "Why don't you just tell her you don't have the energy?"

"Because then I'll feel guilty every time she sees me doing work at someone else's house!" Gary says. "Have you thought any more about taking in one of those Ukrainian refugees? Did you see the news earlier? The government are paying £350 for each one now and Bob and Sarah have already signed up. I think we should do it," Gary seeks to persuade his reluctant wife who knows she'll end up looking after the poor soul as her husband is out most of the time.

"Well, you know that Bob and

Sarah don't really have other commitments and they have the time and money to spare...." she trails off as she can't think of another excuse.

"Come on love. Let's do our bit. We can just offer to take a single woman if you'd rather. That would be easier for you." Gary knows he will win in the end as his wife is a soft touch. He does love her for it but he's noticed that she is getting tired earlier these days.

"Ok, then. I'll do the application tomorrow whilst you're at the golf." Janet secretly wonders whether her husband would be so keen on this grand gesture if Bob and Sarah weren't already signed up, but she's gotten used to Gary's determination to keep up with the Jones's and has convinced herself that his heart's in the right place...most of the time.

# Chapter 2

Gary takes a swing on the golf course. He's getting good at this. Of course, he's only here because his dear friend Richard has recently had surgery and this is part of his recuperation.

"Great shot, mate," Richard says enthusiastically. *He's* only here because he's just had surgery and wants to be as far away from his nagging wife as possible.

"Yeah, really good hit but I'll better it," Jack says. He's taking part because his wife has gone to the Canaries for a week with her girlfriends and he's by himself.

The three men make their way around the course slowly. None of them are particularly good at the sport but they all slap each other on the back, cheer each other on and try to outmanoeuvre each other in equal measure. It's easy to support an underdog, but when one of them starts to win, well, everything changes.

The men finish the course. Jack wins, but only just. Gary thinks its because Jack was using a more expensive club. Richard thinks he just got lucky. All three are sure their individual skills are superior but they keep quiet, apart from Jack who revels in his victory.

They make their way to the bar in the club house and settle in for the rest of the afternoon. Gary briefly thinks of Janet at home probably juggling the housework with the elderly neighbour he had invited round for coffee and now the application to host a Ukrainian. Well, they're a tag team and he's doing his bit by helping out Richard.

"What about the war in Ukraine?" Jack comments as they sip their beer.

"Funny you should mention it. I've just decided to take in some of those refugees," Gary is pleased about this early opportunity to let his friends know of his plans.

Richard looks worried, "But, didn't your daughter in law just die suddenly? Don't your own family need your attention at the moment?"

Gary flushes and hesitates, "Well she did, but we've had the funeral and there's not much I can do for them right now. Dean just needs to be out and about with his buddies, Grant's joined the Jesus people and Sophie seems like she might be going that way as well. I'll be there for them when they're ready, but for now, there's others that need help. You've got a big place. Aren't you going to sign up?"

Now, it's Jack's turn to look awkward. "Well, we've thought about it yeah. Maybe we'll do it soon." He doesn't want to commit to anything as his wife is very much in control and she will be furious if, when she gets back from holiday, he's signed them up for something like this. His wife and

Ukrainian refugees, somehow he can't see it.

"Wait, so Grant and Sophie have both got serious about God, they're haven't joined those "born agains" have they??" Richard offers a subject change. "How on earth did that happen?"

"I don't really know what's happened. I mean, I'm a Christian of course, but Grant seemed pretty crazy at the funeral talking about Hell and judgement and practically begging people to listen. I think Sophie was upset by what he said. I'm hoping it's just a phase, or perhaps a way of dealing with the sadness of losing their mum."

Gary tries to sound appropriately accommodating but inwardly he's pretty annoyed by the change in his grandchildren, particularly Grant. He had had a weak moment at the funeral himself, but that was all it was, a weak moment. Now, he's fully in control of his emotional faculties and doesn't want his family to be known as religious nutcases. Church at Christmas, Easter and Remembrance Day is enough for now.

"Yeah, that's probably all it is. Kids need to believe their dead parents are somewhere even if they're not, it's harmless enough," Jack comments vaguely.

The others just look at him lost in their own thoughts.

# Chapter 3

Janet rushes around preparing tea and answering the phone which rings constantly with people wanting to speak to Gary. She is just in the middle of another phone call with an elderly man whose wife has been rushed into hospital, when the doorbell rings. She stretches the phone cord as far as it will reach and opens the door.

"Oh hi Mrs Yale. Oh, you're on the phone. I'll just come in and wait, shall I?" Mrs Dranty smiles sweetly and heads in through the open door before Janet can reply.

"Yes, sorry, I'm still here Mr Fordy. I was just answering the door. I'll ask Gary to call you when he gets in, he's out at the moment." Janet tries to reassure the distressed old man and then hangs up to attend to her visitor.

She leans against the kitchen wall and sighs, willing herself to summon the energy for a few hours of nonsensical chatter with the lonely Mrs Dranty who has started popping round regularly in recent weeks. She's sure her husband must have encouraged the visitation but he says he only mentioned it once in passing and wasn't expecting her to take him up on it.

"Tea or coffee?" Janet calls through to Mrs Dranty who has already made herself comfortable in their lounge and is busily flicking through a magazine on the coffee table.

"What's that dear? Tea and some cake if you've got it. That would be lovely," Mrs Dranty replies.

"Sure, coming right up." Janet puts the kettle on then searches frantically for anything resembling cake and finds a plastic tub with the remnants of a fruit cake in the pantry. She sniffs it and looks at it. It'll have to do. She cuts a crumbling slice and puts it on a plate. She makes the tea.

"Here we are," Janet puts the tray

on the coffee table and sits down for what she knows will be a long chat.

"Gary not here? That's a shame, I really needed to see him about my lawn and some other bits…but I know he's busy."

"He's with a friend that's just had surgery, I'm afraid," Janet dutifully omits the fact that they are playing golf as she knows her husband prefers for people not to think of him frittering away his precious time.

"Always helping everyone. You're very lucky to have such a husband. I saw him the other day driving a mini bus with a load of scruffy looking kids in the back," Mrs Dranty says this as if looking for an explanation for Gary's association with these ragged children.

"Yes, he drives for Kids Club, it's a special needs charity, twice a week, as a volunteer," Janet ensures she includes the fact it's unpaid.

"Oh, that makes sense," Mrs

Dranty relaxes and smiles. "I'll bet they'll be rolling out the red carpet when he finally reaches the Pearly Gates."

"What? Well, he's only 65!!" Janet exclaims. She resists the urge to tell Mrs Dranty what it's really like living with a husband who is always helping other people and who frequently expects her to do the same.

Mrs Dranty sips her tea and eats her cake carefully. "Well, my late husband was exactly the same, always helping people, nothing was too much trouble, he always….."

Janet's eyes have glazed over and she has tuned out. She is exhausted. She snaps abruptly back to the conversation a few minutes later and finds she is being asked a question.

"So, do you think it's possible?"

"Yes?" Janet replies with no idea what she is agreeing to. She can hardly tell the older woman that she had bored her into zombie mode and that she had fallen asleep with her eyes open.

"Great. I'll expect him tomorrow morning." Mrs Dranty rises and hands her empty cup and plate to Janet who thinks she catches a gleeful glint in the older woman's eye, as she makes for the front door. Her plan has worked perfectly and it only took her 30 minutes.

"Should he bring any tools?" Janet guesses she's just roped her husband into some sort of garden work because Mrs Dranty had earlier mentioned the lawn.

"Just for measuring the space initially. You know, to make sure the new bathroom will fit." Mrs Dranty calls as she closes the front door behind her.

Janet collapses back onto the sofa. Gary will be furious. He has told her repeatedly not to make arrangements on his behalf as he wants to cherry pick his jobs.

In their own house, things have remained broken for a long time and she has been forced to accept that her husband is too busy to address them. It's a small price to pay for being married to someone so well thought of in their local community though. At least this is what she tells herself whenever she feels overwhelmed and lonely.

Janet rehearses her speech in her head. "I think she's getting dementia, as I didn't agree to that." Even as she thinks of it, she knows Mrs Dranty is far too switched on for her to get away with this. In fact, it wouldn't surprise Janet to have learned that Mrs Dranty may have had a recording device to capture their agreement in evidence.

Janet feels weary as she stares at the wall before longingly looking at her neglected knitting in a basket in the corner. She suddenly remembers the application for the Ukrainian refugee that she'd agreed to do. She fires up their ancient computer. She really hates doing stuff online, but it seems to be the way everything operates now. Just as she has found the website and begun reading the pages of instructions for completing the form, the phone rings, as she goes to answer it, the doorbell sounds again……

# Chapter 4

"Did you get to see Dean in the end?" Janet asks Gary.

They are having a rare coffee together at home before Gary needs to address the promise his wife had inadvertently made to Mrs Dranty yesterday afternoon. Janet had explained what had happened and Gary had taken it well. Together they'd decided that the most straight forward course of action was for Gary to measure for the new bathroom, then for them both to order it with Mrs Dranty's credit card. Then, Gary would explain that he didn't have insurance to do the fitting, so she would need to get builders in. In fact, he had already contacted a friend of his who charged a fair price and would do a good job.

"I've tried calling him a few times and I actually went round there earlier. He doesn't answer the phone and

Sophie was the only one at home when I arrived," Gary tells her.

"Did she say anything about how Dean is? Was she okay?" Janet is anxious about her son's family as they haven't really spoken since the upset at the funeral. They've all just returned to their lives before the tragedy as if nothing has happened.

"Actually, she looked really tired and her eyes were red and puffy. I think she'd been crying. She said her dad hasn't been around much and she's worried about his drinking," Gary relays.

"You know what, I really think it would be good for us to have her here for a while. What do you think, love?" Janet asks.

"I thought you weren't sure if you could manage a Ukrainian but now you want to add someone else to our household?!" Gary says, astonished.

"It's hardly the same and she's our granddaughter. I just don't think she's going to get any support from

Dean for a while and Grant will be off with his church friends. I know Sophie was interested in the church stuff but I'm not sure if it will stick and she's probably pretty lonely. Being 14 is difficult enough without suddenly losing your mother," Janet reasons.

"Well, if you think you can take her on, sure. It'll make the tutoring easier as well. She can help with the Ukrainians when they arrive, take her mind off the trauma. It'll also be good for Dean not to have to worry about parenting as he recovers from what's happened," Gary agrees with her suggestion. He and Janet are both retired teachers and he has been tutoring Sophie in the classes she struggles with, Science and Maths, for a while now.

"Great, I'll text her and see what she says," Janet reaches for her phone and sends a quick message to Sophie asking her to give her a call when she can. Her grand children find it hilarious that she does this; texts someone asking them to call her, rather than just passing on the message in the text. It's a generational thing and Janet prefers talking to texting.

Gary heads off to Mrs Dranty's house.

"Let me know how it goes. Fingers crossed," Janet calls after him. She feels guilty for getting him into this, but feels sure he can get out of it without Mrs Dranty thinking any less of him. After all, everyone knows you need appropriate insurance to do a big job like fitting a bathroom.

Janet hears the noise of her phone ringing. It's Sophie.

"Hi sweetie, are you okay?" she asks her grand daughter.

"I'm okay Gran," Sophie's voice is quiet on the other end of the line. She doesn't sound okay.

"Granddad said when he came round that he thought you might have been crying," Janet gently prompts.

Sophie bursts into tears.

"Oh Gran, it's been awful. I'm really worried about my dad and I don't know what to do," Sophie sobs.

"You shouldn't have to worry about him darling. You're grieving yourself. How's your brother?"

"He seems okay, he's got his church mates although he's been staying in his room a lot and he's also worried about Dad," Sophie tells her Gran.

"Well, me and Granddad have talked it over and we'd like you to come and stay with us for a bit, if you'd like? It'll give your dad a chance to sort himself out and Grant will be okay."

"Really, I'd love that!" Sophie perks up and brightens just at the thought of somewhere new and different rather than the depressing house which seems empty without her mother.

"Just so you know, we're also applying to host a Ukrainian, so you might have to share some space but you'll have your own room," Janet encourages her.

"That's fine. I think it's great that you're doing that. They really need help," Sophie observes.

Janet heart goes out to her granddaughter who is so kind hearted that she is thinking of others despite having just lost her mum.

"Well, look, get some things together and we'll come and pick you up a bit later. Don't worry if you forget things as we can always drop by and grab them, it's only 10 minutes in the car," Janet says.

"Are you sure? Wait, what about Dad?"

"I'll talk to him, but I'm pretty sure he'll be glad that you are being taken care of as I don't think he's up to it, sweetie."

"You're probably right." Sophie recalls her drunken father crawling in from another night with his mates. "See you later then."

# Chapter 5

Gary sighs as he leaves Mrs Dranty's house. The hasty plan he and his wife had conducted had gone almost perfectly, but he still feels bad. He had seen the brief look of sadness and disappointment in their elderly neighbour's eyes as she had reassured him that of course she understood that he couldn't do the job himself without the correct insurance.

He feels guilty for lying and senses that Mrs Dranty knew that if he had really wanted to do it, he could have; where there's a will there's a way.

But, where would it end? If he fitted Mrs Dranty's bathroom, Gary feels sure that all of his neighbours would expect the same consideration, so unless he's planning on getting a job as a full time plumber, he's justified in refusing.

Gary arrives home, he's tired just

from the visit and the lengthy explanations he'd given to Mrs Dranty. Janet is on the phone.

"Oh, yes. I'm so sorry Mr Fordy. Gary hasn't forgotten. We just had a family emergency to deal with. I'll get him to call you very soon." Janet turns as she hears the front door opening and shrugs at her husband as he comes in. She hangs up.

"I know you've only just got in, but I told Mr Fordy you'd call him yesterday, Bertha was rushed into hospital and I don't think he can get there by himself," Janet tells him.

"I just need a few minutes to sit down," Gary collapses into the nearest chair and within minutes is fast asleep.

3 hours later the phone rings again.

"Oh no," Janet mutters as she answers it. "I'll just get him, Mr Fordy, yes, he's just got in. I think I can hear him in the garage actually, give me a few seconds."

"Wake up Gary. It's Mr Fordy," she whispers urgently as she shakes her husband awake.

"What, hmmm. Five more minutes," Gary mumbles.

"No, it's Mr Fordy, you HAVE to talk to him now," Janet insists.

Gary rubs his eyes and tries to focus. "What? Okay, hand me the phone."

Janet obliges.

"Hello, Mr Fordy. I'm so sorry I didn't call you back earlier, you see I was…."

The old man is crying on the other end of the line.

"Mr Fordy?" Gary says.

Through choked sobs, Mr Fordy simply says, "Bertha died."

Gary is deflated and for once in his life, speechless. He has no idea how to comfort the grieving Mr Fordy. He has no bright ideas, no platitudes that wouldn't sound empty and no hope to offer. He wishes he had called Mr Fordy back earlier and offered him a lift to see his dying wife. Guilt threatens to overwhelm him whilst his own mind is trying to alleviate his conscience by listing all the other things he had had to do.

"Mr Fordy, I'll come round straight away." Gary manages the only thing he can think of. Perhaps, he can help arrange the funeral, or get the man some groceries or something. He knows it won't be enough.

Several hours later, Gary arrives home.

"How was poor Mr Fordy?" Janet asks sympathetically. She hadn't gone with her husband fearing the two of them might be too much for him at this difficult time.

"Oh, it was awful," Gary says. His wife notices that he is pale and his face looks drawn like a man in shock. "I had no idea Bertha was at risk of dying. Did you realise how serious it was?"

"Not really, I mean he did say she had been rushed into hospital but he wasn't specific and I assumed he would have made it sound more urgent…I guess he didn't want to bother us?" Janet feels teary at the thought of Mr Fordy not getting the chance to say goodbye to his wife because they hadn't responded to his pleas in time.

"All I could do was sit with him as he told me how he met Bertha and all about their lives together but he kept crying so it was difficult to hear him. It was worse because he didn't even mention the fact he hadn't got to the hospital. He was just very grateful that I'd come round and kept saying he knew I was a busy man." Gary shakes his head. "Then, he was rambling about Bertha being in a better place and asking me if I was sure that she was in Heaven. Obviously, I reassured the man best I could but I felt completely and totally useless. This must never happen again."

"You can't do everything for

everyone, dear. I'm sure you did your best," Janet says soothingly.

The phone rings and Janet answers it.

"Gran, I've been waiting for hours. You did mean today, didn't you?" Sophie asks.

"Oh! Hang on, love. Yes, I did mean today. One of our neighbours just lost his wife and we've been dealing with that. Your granddad will come and get you now," Janet looks to Gary who sighs and nods wearily.

"It's just, I told Dad about it and he didn't believe that's where I was going," Sophie says.

"I was planning to talk to him beforehand, but I can do it when I get there," Gary says.

Janet relays the information to Sophie and hangs up.

"Another person we forgot and this time it's our own flesh and blood," Gary looks downcast as he gets to his feet and heads for the door.

"Sophie won't mind, but you will need to pacify Dean now. He'll probably make a fuss that we went behind his back and made the offer to her before discussing it with him. He's a bit like that these days," Janet comments.

"Oh, joy. I'm not sure I've got the energy for this," Gary responds.

"Perhaps, if you use a bit of reverse psychology on him. I'm sure he could do with a break and not having to worry about Sophie but try and make it seem like it's his idea rather than a cunning scheme that he's been left out of," Janet suggests.

"I'll do my best."

Dean answers the door to his dad. He looks a little annoyed but not furious.

Gary heads inside and is nearly knocked out by the strong smell of bleach in the kitchen.

"What is that smell?"

"Oh, I had to clean as a curry fell on the floor and it really stank," Dean says innocently.

Something doesn't seem to add up, but Gary hasn't time to figure it out and he needs to sort out Sophie.

"Hey, so you know a while ago, you suggested that Sophie stayed with us for a few days a week so she could get more done when I'm tutoring her?" Gary begins.

"Yeah, that was ages ago, though," Dean scratches his head.

Gary notices the dark circles under his son's eyes and that he seems to be struggling for words.

"We thought we'd do it now. I tried to come by and talk to you the other day but you weren't here." Gary hopes Dean doesn't ask for specifics as he doesn't have any.

Dean appears to be focusing on something else. His eyes are looking around as if he is concerned that his father might see something that he would rather remained hidden.

"Oh, okay. Yeah, sounds good.

She's upstairs." Dean indicates the staircase.

Gary hears the slur in Dean's speech and realises that he's trying to limit his words. He moves a step closer and Dean nearly falls over backwards as he seeks to maintain the distance between them. Gary smells the alcohol and suddenly the picture, including the bleach smell, is clear.

"You really need…", Gary starts but doesn't finish his sentence. He's there to get Sophie. Getting into a confrontation with his son about his drinking will not help. He changes tack, "to call Sophie. Does she know I'm here?" Gary says. Somehow, the fact that his son doesn't seem to notice his change of direction, or that he's seen the alcohol, makes him feel sad.

Sophie appears on the stairs with a large bag over her shoulder.

Dean looks relieved as he says goodbye to his daughter. He doesn't ask how long she will be going for.

"Where's Grant?" Gary asks as an afterthought.

"You taking him as well?" Dean asks with a trace of irritation.

"He's out with church friends," Sophie replies quickly, sensing an argument brewing.

"No, of course not, I just haven't seen him for a while," Gary clarifies.

They head outside to the car. As they are loading Sophie's stuff, she looks back to the house and sees her dad standing in the kitchen staring blankly out of the window.

"How long has he been like that?" Gary asks once they are in the car.

"Pretty much since Mum died with the odd break. That's not bad actually. He's just hung over," Sophie says quietly.

"I smelt alcohol, so he's had a drink today," Gary says. "And what's with the bleach?"

"He came in drunk last night with some mates I think. The whole place was covered in bottles and cans this morning and absolutely reeked of booze and cigarettes," Sophie almost whispers the explanation. Even though she's speaking to her granddad, she feels humiliated and embarrassed by her father's recent behaviour.

"I'm sorry you've been dealing with that, love. You won't catch me or your grandma behaving like that, I assure you." Gary winks but his joke falls flat.

Sophie isn't really listening anyway. She is conscious that with every mile they travel they get further away from her family home. She sighs with relief as she feels the weight of responsibility for her father lifting.

# Chapter 6

"I was on the phone to Gordon earlier and he's running for his town council." Gary, who is in the lounge, calls to Janet in the kitchen. "I'm thinking maybe I should apply for ours."

Janet stays silent and pulls a face.

"What do you think?" Gary repeats the implied question.

Janet inwardly groans. She's been waiting for something like this to happen. Her husband is already trying to do far too much and she knows the amount of work that would be involved in running for the council. This, not mentioning that they would be even more in the spotlight, which she hates, and expected to live as perfect citizens, always in the public eye.

"Well, isn't there an upper age limit?" Janet asks hopefully.

"Of course not, well not unless you're over 75. It's mostly retired people like us who have the time," Gary replies confidently. He's already been researching the role.

Janet's hopes that the suggestion was just a throw away idea are fading fast as she realises her husband is serious, and set on the idea.

"Okay, well if that's what you want to do. What are the requirements?" Janet asks hesitantly still hoping Gary won't qualify.

"Well, I need to be involved in the community, a known figure. I already help the neighbours, do the church stuff and drive the mini bus so that's a good start. I need to be involved in local projects and charities. Hopefully the Ukrainian will get here soon now that we've applied." Gary is checking things off a list in an article in front of him.

"Hmm. What else?" Janet says absent-mindedly. She's not bothered about the things Gary already does, it's the big changes that she's worried about.

"Well, I'll probably need to go to more meetings about local issues and maybe try and get in the papers a bit more. I might even be able to get a column or something," Gary says vaguely.

"What would you write about?" Janet asks. Her husband may be helpful and productive, but he's not known for his journalistic skills. Indeed, she's never known him to express any type of interest in anything of the sort before. He reads *The Daily Mail* each day and that's the extent of it.

"Oh, I don't know. Local events. How hard can it be?"

"Very, if you don't have a clear plan or vision for what you want to communicate," Janet says firmly. She being the retired English teacher with Gary's expertise mainly in Science and Maths, can already see where this is leading.

"Oh. This one could be more difficult. Respect for diversity, including the various faiths. The person who wrote this article suggests attending services for all of the major faiths at least once a month and making sure they are the largest and most visible representations in the community," Gary says.

"Hmm, won't your work at the drop in cover that?" Janet asks.

"I don't think so as it's not really a religious service and the church is tiny. I'd probably need to find another one. Which other religions do you think I'd need to think about?"

Sophie joins their conversation having entered the room. "Islam, obviously and probably Hinduism and Buddhism. You're listing the major religions, right?"

"Well, yes, but only the ones that have a good number in the UK and that hold services that I can attend," Gary says to his granddaughter. "I'm thinking of running for the town council."

"Well, you could come to church with me, but I'm not sure you'd like it."

Sophie laughs as she imagines her grandparents standing amongst the strobe lights in the darkened room as the worship band creates the atmosphere.

Janet laughs nervously.

"Wait, I've had a great idea!" Gary exclaims. "Why don't we go to the Parish church where they had the funeral?"

"We, you mean I'd have to go as well?" Janet says. "But, Sunday is my rest day, I love being able to chill out with a late start and a good book."

"Darling, if I run for the council, it'll need to be a joint effort. How many councillors appear without their devoted partners by their side?"

"I guess you're right," Janet agrees reluctantly. "Are you sure it's worth it though. You already do a lot for people."

Gary isn't listening. He's already planning his take over of the council. He's looking up the attendance statistics at the Parish church to make sure it's central and has the largest congregation.

"Don't you need a nomination for that type of thing?" Sophie is fiddling with her phone but casually listening to her grandparents conversation. "It says here that to become a councillor you'll need at least 10 nominations from people that aren't related to you. It doesn't really make sense as how many people wake up and think, 'I'll nominate this person for town council today'?"

"I think you have to canvass and try to persuade people to nominate you, honey," Janet points out.

"Oh, how awkward. I'd hate that," Sophie flushes.

"Well, your granddad has plenty of locals who'd be happy to support him, I'm sure, but yes it does feel a little uncomfortable." Janet looks uncertain about the whole idea.

Gary had been quiet as he made his plans but he's tuned back into the conversation. "I'll ask some of the neighbours and folks at the drop in, then there's the mini bus staff. I hope I don't have to ask Mr Fordy, but if necessary…."

"Oh no!" Janet gasps. "You can't possibly do that. The poor man."

"You're probably right," Gary concedes "But if needs must."

Janet busies herself preparing food. She is horrified that her husband would even consider prevailing upon the widowed Mr Fordy especially as they had totally failed to help him in his hour of need. She had hoped never to have to cross paths with the man again fearing the pained expressions and broken hearted retelling of stories about his wife that Gary had described. Gary might be able to deal with it but she knows she cannot.

Gary is determined and once he sets his mind to something he always achieves it. He feels like he deserves some recognition for his hard work since his retirement. Sitting on the town council would be a badge of honour to add to his many achievements. He can't wait to get there and see his name amongst the others on the boards at City Hall. It might even lead to an MBE later down the line.

Gary allows his mind to drift to a fantasy world where he is King, adored and love by everyone.

# Chapter 7

Gary walks out of the blood bank. Things had gone perfectly. He knew that if he timed it right, several acquaintances would be in the queue. After a short chat, he had easily secured two more nominations. That makes nine.

He gets in his car and heads home whistling cheerfully. He slows as he nears the house of Mr Fordy. Only one more nomination and Mr Fordy had been so very grateful on his last visit. The words of his wife pop into his head. He feels a touch of guilt but time has already healed the bulk of it and he's forgotten how terrible he had felt after his last visit. He shakes the remnants off as he pulls his car over and gets out. He heads towards the front door. He rings the bell.

Mr Fordy takes a while to answer the door.

"Oh it's you, Mr Yale. Come in,

come in," Mr Fordy smiles with his mouth but there is pain behind his eyes.

Gary notices that his neighbour has aged significantly and that he is wearing a stained shirt. He follows Mr Fordy inside his house and observes the state of the kitchen before Mr Fordy quickly closes the door on it. Bowls and plates with half eaten food are strewn around and a smell emanating. Gary decides it's none of his business unless Mr Fordy asks for help. It would be rude to point it out when Mr Fordy had clearly not wanted him to see it. Besides, it would be an ongoing job which Gary really doesn't have time for. He'll talk to Janet later about tactfully suggesting a cleaner.

They head into the lounge.

"Tea or coffee?" Mr Fordy asks.

"I'm actually okay, I've just had one," Gary lies. A white lie as he wants to spare the old man the embarrassment of dirty cups, or a poorly made beverage. "I just came to check that you were doing okay?" Another lie but he can hardly make his request without some polite chit chat.

"Well, Bertha and I would usually be having coffee about now and it's difficult to face things without her. I remember....."

Gary tunes out as Mr Fordy starts reminiscing once again. He needs to find a subtle way to bring this discussion back to his reason for being here. He remembers some advice he's recently read in a self help book; try to relate the thing you want to talk about to something that is important to the person you're talking to. Mr Fordy is obviously only interested in his late wife Bertha. That is the point of connection. Suddenly, Gary has a brain wave.

"So, Bertha's funeral is next week, you said?" Gary abruptly cuts into Mr Fordy's stream of consciousness.

The old man's face lights up at the mention of his wife but quickly darkens at the reference to her funeral.

"Yes, next Tuesday."

"Is everything planned already? I mean, do you need any help organising any of the speakers or anything?" Gary asks.

"Well our children have done most of it but it has been difficult as they live so far away," Mr Fordy tells him. "I say, would you like to say anything?"

Gary flushes. "Really? I'd be honoured. I could talk about her love of the garden and how we all used to sit outside with a coffee after I'd mowed the lawn."

"Well she did love the garden, but her main passion was reading, she loved poetry. Maybe I can find one of her favourites for you to read," Mr Fordy replies.

"That's very personal, might be better coming from a family member," Gary quickly suggests. "I just remember that she loved the smell of the cut grass and the way the birds twittered in the hedgerow after it had been pruned."

"That's true and she definitely appreciated all the work you did for us. We both recognise that you are a busy man," Mr Fordy says.

Gary takes a breath then goes for it.

"She once said to me that I should run for town council," Gary cringes despite himself. Bertha hadn't quite said this. She'd actually said that she knew someone like Gary who was always helping people who had become a Neighbourhood Watch coordinator. Still, it's not a big leap.

"Oh. She didn't say that to me but it might not be a bad idea. Is it something you've been thinking about then?" Mr Fordy says. He's interested in any of his late wife's wishes, however obscure and irrelevant they may appear.

"Maybe. I think I'd need to be nominated though," Gary says as if he's not really thought it through.

"Well, I know that Bertha was always worried about the speed the cars around here travelled, especially on the stretch of road just outside our house. Would you be able to do something about that if you became a councillor," Mr Fordy asks.

Gary smiles. It wasn't too difficult after all. "Yes, of course. We could also place a bench on the green across the road in her memory if you think she would have liked that?"

Mr Fordy's eyes fill with tears.

Gary feels awkward. He doesn't mention that he plans to use the laying of the bench as a way of drawing attention to his campaign for the council. He knows it will be easy enough to get his own name on the plaque next to Bertha's as the funder and facilitator as he's seen them before.

"So, I'll pop a nomination form in the post for you. I can fill it in for you if you'd like and then you can just sign it?" Gary says. He's already standing up to leave.

Mr Fordy looks confused, "Wait,

oh, okay. Yes, that's fine. So, are you going to say anything at the funeral next week?"

"I think it would be better if your family did that. I'll definitely be there though," Gary offers. He's thought better of speaking at the funeral fearing that one of Mr Fordy's children might be suspicious of his motivations; swooping in out of nowhere and giving a form of eulogy when they've never even met him. Besides, he's got what he came for and doesn't want to go overboard. He says goodbye and heads home.

Now for dealing with his wife who he knows will be furious or maybe, he won't tell her. What she doesn't know can't hurt her and she won't care when he gets elected and becomes Councillor Yale.

# Chapter 8

Nominations received. Gary is in the running. Janet is even starting to catch the vision and is busying herself with the campaign. Only Sophie seems bemused by the whole idea. She had been even more so when, for the first time in living memory, her grandparents had gotten up early on Sunday and headed to the Parish church.

Afterwards, they had discussed the fantastic building and huge number of prominent people in attendance. Gary had used the opportunity to network and let people know about his campaign.

The vicar, who they had recognised from Annie's funeral, had even been persuaded to allow them to place a flier on the church bulletin board. Gary had pointed out that it wasn't really about politics, but doing good things in the community and helping people. The vicar was very much in favour of these things. In fact, his short sermon had been on that very subject which had definitely helped Gary in his endeavour.

The vicar had flushed slightly when Gary had initially introduced himself and he had made the connection to the recent funeral that he had led. He recalled the urgent young man who had invaded his platform with a grim message of judgement and damnation before he had managed to restore order by moving to the next hymn as quickly as possible.

However, Gary had apologised for his grandson, Grant's "inappropriate outburst" blaming it on overwhelming grief over his mother and assuring the vicar that Grant had since calmed down and reflected on his behaviour. He promised that he would arrange for Grant to apologise himself at some point in the not too distant future knowing that this wouldn't be necessary as it would all be forgotten by then. Just as well, as Grant definitely wouldn't be up for apologising as he still seemed as fanatical as ever.

Still, the situation had been smoothed over with Gary ensuring he made a large public contribution to the collection plate that was passed around. He had achieved his goal and become buddies with another important community figure. He'd even arranged a round of golf, not on Sunday of course, but for later in the week.

Helpfully, through his multi-faith connections, the vicar had also pointed Gary in the right direction for services and gatherings of the Muslims, Buddhists and Hindus. The latter meeting in an upper room in the church each week. In fact, some of the vicar's congregation attended these meetings to learn more about other faiths. The vicar was keen to point out that he intended to get to one in due course and that they had discussed having joint meetings occasionally on a Sunday. But, this had been narrowly voted down by the congregation and someone had sent an anonymous message to the Bishop who had made it clear that such collaborations wouldn't be tolerated under the current C of E regulations.

Gary is pleased that he can kill two birds with one stone by getting involved in this Parish church and congratulates himself on his bright idea of attending in the first place.

# Chapter 9

"Did you know you were in the news?" Sophie calls.

"Really, which paper?" Gary asks.

"No, I mean online, the local news on Google," Sophie answers as if it's obvious.

"Oh. What does it say?"

"Just that you've been nominated for town council but it describes you as a prominent figure in the local community as well as a church goer and supporter of other faiths." Sophie laughs. "Yeah, for all of five minutes. And it says here that you've taken in a Ukrainian family. Who are the sources I wonder?"

"Actually, I was asked to write it myself," Gary admits shamefacedly. "But they must've edited it. I said we had applied to host a Ukrainian but I didn't mention a family and didn't say they had arrived, obviously."

"I hope they don't dig into your background and find out you've only just started some of these things. That would be really embarrassing," Sophie says.

"I doubt they'll bother, hon, it's only the local council. Not the office of Prime Minister!" Gary laughs now.

"It's a bit like an MP though isn't it?" asks Janet as she joins their discussion.

"A bit, but on a much lower level and more about the community than politics," Gary says. He really doesn't know the difference but his family don't need to know that.

"I hope you don't have any skeletons in your closet Granddad as I'd hate for all that to be out in public," Sophie worries. "You know, there was an important woman last year who had been speeding but she said she wasn't driving. The police proved she had been and she ended up getting sent to prison!"

"Woah, slow down Soph. I

would never do anything like that and it was because she lied and said her husband had been driving, so she was convicted of attempting to pervert the course of justice. She wasn't sent to prison just for speeding," Gary explains. Even as he does so, he remembers including his wife on his car insurance even though she never drives his car as it brought the premium down significantly, and occasionally bringing printer paper home from work when they had run out. These things are not the same though and Gary pushes them out of his mind.

"What about all the drama when you were suspended after that boy said you'd grabbed his arm?" Janet recalls.

"It wasn't proven and the allegation was dropped, you know that, sweetheart," Gary responds.

"I know, but his parents did move him to another school and I think they're still local. You don't think they'll bring it up again when your name's in circulation?" Janet looks anxious.

Gary thinks back to the incident where he had lost his temper with the trouble maker and grabbed his arm leaving a red mark. "Of course not, it was ages ago. If they do, I'll just do what I did then, deny it which is the truth anyway." Gary has become so used to his version of events that it almost feels like he is telling the truth, at least that's what he's convinced himself. His conscience occasionally rears its head but he shoves it back in its box where it belongs.

The phone rings and Janet reaches to answer it.

"Oh hello Mrs Dranty. Oh, they've arrived have they? That's good. Yes, you saw his name in the paper. Thankyou for the nomination, he really appreciates it. No, I'm afraid he's not available at the moment. Yes, okay, no problem." Janet hangs up and turns to Gary who had signalled that he didn't want to speak to their neighbour.

"What did she want?" Gary asks.

"The builders have arrived and she saw your name on the list in the paper. I think she just wanted to let you know that she's going away for a few days as the water will be disconnected. You really should talk to her when she calls next time or go and see her when she's back," Janet encourages. "You need her on side."

"I will, but I don't want to get roped into the building work, or asked to collect supplies or something. You know she'll have me doing little jobs if I go near the place before the work is finished," Gary points out. "She's probably left me a 'to do' list on the fridge!"

"Fair enough, but she's away for now so when the job's done you should get round there. You know what she's like. You don't want her to go off you and start babbling that she nominated you but you've shown no interest in her ever since!" Janet replies.

"Yes dear," Gary says absent mindedly.

# Chapter 10

Gary and Sophie head for the front door.

"Where are you going love?" Janet asks.

"I'm going to drive the bus, they changed the day this week because of the bank holiday," Gary answers.

"No, I know about you. I meant Sophie?" Janet says.

"I'm just going to see a friend," Sophie replies vaguely.

"Okay, make sure you're home by ten please sweet," Janet instructs. They barely see their granddaughter these days. It's been several months since she moved in and she's no bother but she isn't around a lot and Janet doesn't really know what she's up to. They've just been so busy getting the campaign up and running.

"Sure, see you later," Sophie

says. Moving in with her grandparents has given her freedoms she didn't even know existed and she's enjoying being independent.

Sophie walks to the bus stop and Gary gets the car out of the garage. He's not quick enough though and Mrs Harma calls his name from across the road. Gary has stopped deliberately lingering outside his house in order to be visibly helpful to his neighbours as he has been inundated with requests recently.

"Hi Mrs Harma, I'm just going out, driving the bus for those kids." Gary calls as he tries to head off the conversation but Mrs Harma comes bustling over. She looks worried.

"It's just, you know you said to leave the back garden for the wildlife?"

"Yes, it's lovely isn't it. We enjoy ours," Gary gushes.

"Well, yes, but Roy and Joan are complaining about one of the plants encroaching on their garden. They want me to cut it down as they say it's illegal or something…Could you take a look?" Mrs Harma pleads.

"Let me look later, but I'm sure it's nothing serious," Gary reassures her.

"They used a name big hogweed, I think it was?" Mrs Harma says.

Gary spins around to face her, "Giant hogweed?? Are you sure? Oh dear. Now don't touch it okay?"

"Well I tried pulling it out earlier, but couldn't manage it," Mrs Harma confesses. "What will happen?"

"Did you wear gloves?" Gary asks urgently.

"Of course," Mrs Harma says "But I've been feeling a bit itchy and my hands and arms are all red now." She shows her sore arms to Gary.

"Go and have a bath or shower and change your clothes. You really need to get any bits of the plant off you. It's really quite dangerous," Gary advises. He knows all about this plant and the damage it can cause.

Mrs Harma looks petrified.

"What will it do. You're frightening me."

"I'll go and get Janet. I really have to go," Gary says.

He knocks on his own front door, explains things to his wife and reminds her that Mrs Harma has nominated him, then leaves her to deal with the situation as he heads off to drive the bus.

"Oh, if only I'd known that this plant was dangerous. I would have got rid of it or got it sorted out before it got so big," Mrs Harma moans to Janet.

"Tell you what, you really need to go and have a shower and change as Gary said. I'll have a look in your garden whilst you're doing that and we'll see what we can do. How's that?"Janet asks.

"Okay, my arms are itching so maybe a shower will help."

Janet wanders around to their neighbour's back garden as Mrs Harma heads indoors for a shower.

Janet gasps when she sees the totally overgrown and unmanageable state of the forest that has sprung up across the road. How had they not realised and why had Gary allowed it to get to this impossible position? She had thought her husband's tricks to get out of dealing with Mrs Harma's lawn were amusing but now, she feels desperately sorry for the old lady, as well as wondering how on earth it can be rectified without costing the earth.

Walking around, she sees a small quantity of the infamous giant hogweed recognisable for its cow parsley like appearance. Then, she sees something even more alarming, a plant she identifies as Japanese knotweed is growing in abundance all across the garden. It has invaded all the other plants and is up against Roy and Joan's fence. No doubt, the roots have already travelled.

Mrs Harma appears beside her, fresh and clean from her shower, although her arms still look swollen.

"Can you see it? Is it that?" She points to the giant hogweed.

"Well, yes, that's a problem. But I'm afraid you've also got Japanese knotweed everywhere," Janet says slowly trying to keep her tone even so as not to alarm her neighbour further.

"Is that bad?" Mrs Harma has no idea.

"It will need removing. Both plants will need to be destroyed as they are invasive and get out of control very quickly," Janet tells her. "You won't be able to do it yourself. It will need specialists with their equipment and chemical sprays."

"Oh no, but what about my wildlife?" Mrs Harma is crestfallen "Will it be expensive?" she asks as an afterthought.

"I'm sorry but your wildlife will probably be taken out with the weeds and yes it will be very expensive." Janet puts her arm around the lady as she delivers the double blow.

"Oh no," Mrs Harma sits down heavily on a garden chair.

"Shall I call an expert and try and get a quote? I can ask whether there's any way to preserve some of your garden," Janet suggests. She already knows what the expert will say; that the garden is way too overgrown and out of control for anything but total obliteration but she wants to give some hope to the old lady whose life is wrapped up in her garden. She hopes she can convince the expert not to hint that if the garden had been taken care of properly in the first place, this may not have been necessary.

"Yes, please do," Mrs Harma says gratefully.

Janet heads back across the road to make the call leaving Mrs Harma to grieve the loss of her pride and joy.

# Chapter 11

"BOOM!" The sound is so loud that Gary and Janet, who had been sipping coffee in their back garden, jump to their feet and automatically look to the sky.

A plume of smoke is rising from a house a few doors down on their side of the street. They rush down their garden path to the front of their house and, joining other residents similarly concerned, run towards the source of the noise.

"WHAT?" Gary exclaims.

Everyone has stopped short of the site. There is a collective disbelief as the residents of Gorse Close stare at the pile of rubble that had been Mrs Dranty's detached house. The smoke and dust linger in the air and there are no recognisable items on display.

Looking around in dismay, Gary sees the builders leaning against a small white van a short distance from the explosion. They had been drinking tea, but their cups are smashed on the ground. They also appear to be in shock and have made no effort to move towards the collapsed building. There is a deathly silence.

"WAS ANYONE IN THERE?" A shout from a neighbour.

"No, the old lady went away for a few days," one of the builder's finds his voice as he continues to stare at the devastation.

"What happened?"

"Is anyone hurt?"

"Has someone called the police?"

"What about the gas board? It must be a gas explosion."

The voices begin to clamour as people demand answers. No explanations are offered. In the confusion, the builders regain their faculties and quietly enter the small white van, then slip almost unnoticed from the scene.

"Wait, don't let them leave."

"Did someone get the registration?"

"Who are they?"

"Who do they work for?"

"Who hired them?"

Gary watches the white van as it reaches the end of the street, then he grabs Janet by the arm and pulls her back along the pavement to their house.

Once inside, he breathes a sigh of relief. "She must've used different builders as they weren't the ones I recommended."

Janet stares at him.

"Really? Is that what you're thinking about right now? What about the danger of the explosion? What about the fact that Mrs Dranty's entire life has just been destroyed in five seconds flat? Sometimes, I don't think I know who you are!"

"Well of course I'm thinking about those things but we know Mrs

Dranty is away, the builders were having a tea break by the look of it and no one was injured. I'd say that's pretty lucky," Gary says, slightly less confidently after being rebuked by his wife.

"So, I guess now it's time to make sure Gary Yale's campaign hasn't been damaged," Janet says in a tone that he hasn't heard before.

"Yes, exactly. Reputation is everything at the moment and things like this could be disastrous if they go the wrong way." Gary hasn't sensed the exasperation in her tone and is oblivious to her feelings on the subject.

"More disastrous than your house exploding resulting in homelessness and possible bankruptcy, not to mention if anyone decides to sue for shock, stress or potential injury? I hope someone has the right insurance…" Janet's voice is rising as she lists the consequences.

Gary is unknowingly treading on thin ice. "Well, no, of course not. I wonder why she didn't use the builders I recommended."

"ENOUGH. Enough about the stupid builders and your worthless campaign. I'm going to go and find out if Mrs Dranty has been told what's happened and make sure the news is broken gently. You can stay here thinking about yourself if you want but I've had enough!" Janet angrily pushes past Gary who is left with his mouth hanging open. He hadn't realised that his wife was angry, make that furious. He's never seen her like this and it scares him.

"Wait! Make sure you tell her that it wasn't the builders I recommended," Gary calls after her. Apparently, he can't help himself.

Janet turns and gives him a look that suggests *she* is about to explode before heading out of the front door.

His wife out of the way, Gary sets about minimising the damage. He calls his builders to find out why they hadn't taken the job.

"Hey Adam, you know that job I offered you, yeah the bathroom at the little old lady's house?" Gary says.

"Oh hi, Gary. Yeah sorry I wasn't there today, I had an appointment. Hope it's all going well, though?"

Gary feels his stomach drop and the bile rising in his throat.

"Wait. So it was your team at the house today?" he manages.

"Well, who else did you think it would be? You gave us the job!" Adam laughs.

"Oh no no no no," Gary moans.

"What's the matter?" Adam says. "Did they arrive late, or spill coffee on someone's carpet?" he laughs again.

"You really don't know?" Gary says. "They blew up the house!!"

There is silence.

"What? What on earth? I hope this is a joke. It's not really funny though mate!" Adam says.

"I'm deadly serious. The whole house exploded then collapsed. Maybe a gas leak. You'd best get on to your insurance asap," Gary advises.

"Wait, was anyone hurt? The boys? Or the lady? Anyone? No, wait, the lady went away didn't she?" Adam starts to panic.

"No one was hurt as far as we could tell. Your lads were on a tea break near their van but it's total destruction city there mate," Gary informs him. "Expensive mistake. How long have those guys been working for you?"

"They're new," Adam admits. "I thought it'd be okay as it was a simple job and I was only gone for a day."

"It gets worse. I don't think they hung around afterwards. They shot off without waiting for the police, or anyone," Gary says.

"Oh man. They probably didn't know what to do and panicked. I'll come over there right now," Adam says.

"Listen mate, I know this probably isn't the right time but is there any way you could keep our association quiet, you know I'm running for the council," Gary asks desperately.

"Seems a little unimportant right now, but sure. I'll pretend I don't know you." Adam shakes his head in disgust as he hangs up.

Janet reaches Mrs Dranty and helps her make arrangements to stay in alternative accommodation. Initially, she had offered for her to stay with them, but Mrs Dranty was reluctant to impose herself. She also seems to have forgotten that it was Gary who had recommended the builders in the first place, at least she doesn't mention it to Janet.

Adam Daily arrives at the scene and assesses the damage. He does have insurance that will cover his worker's incompetence but he is appalled at the mess and shocked by the scale of the destruction. He is relieved that no one was hurt but also realises that it was a close call and he will be forced to dismiss some, or all of his workers. In fact, the insurance claim puts him out of business.

As requested, he doesn't mention his connection with Gary Yale, no matter how tempting it might be to put a permanent spanner in the works of his acquaintance's campaign.

# Chapter 12

Over the next few months, the settlement is agreed, the house is rebuilt and Mrs Dranty moves in to a new-build with all the mod cons that she had been lacking before. She seems pleased with the arrangement, the insurance even having footed the hotel bill as she had nowhere else to stay. She doesn't like the colour of her front door but that's a small price to pay in the big scheme of things.

Meanwhile, Mrs Harma, with Janet's help, has had the council round to do extensive work in her garden. Due to her low income it has all been done for free. The giant hogweed and Japanese knotweed have been destroyed (for now) and there is some wildlife left. They have planted some new species and she is eagerly awaiting their growth in the Spring.

Ron and Joan, next door, are satisfied that she didn't intentionally allow her weeds to overrun her garden and are happy that the situation has now been resolved. They are all on good terms once again.

Mr Fordy is pleased when the promised bench in memory of his late wife Bertha appears on the green opposite his house. He notes that the name of Gary Yale looms large beside it, but he's sure this was probably a legal requirement documenting the funding source. He often sits on the bench reminiscing about his late wife. Nothing has been done about the speeding in his road, but he assumes this will happen if, and when Gary becomes Councillor Yale.

None of them have seen or heard from Gary since he secured their nominations. He seems to have disappeared completely. None of them really blame him for the various calamities that have befallen them, but they do sometimes wonder whether he is really the trustworthy individual he makes himself out to be.

They also wonder whether they should have been so quick to nominate him for the local council. They all follow the local news and are aware that the election will be held very soon. Having previously been rooting for Gary, they now feel indifferent about the result.

# Chapter 13

Gary sits at home. He is nervously awaiting the election result.

He decides to check their joint email account once again. There are no new messages but he does notice something in the draft folder that hadn't been there before. He opens it. It's an application to host a Ukrainian. Gary is confused. Why is this in his draft folder, it was sent months ago. Wasn't it?

"Janet, can you come here for a second?" Gary calls.

Janet has long since calmed down after her furious exit to clear up her husband's mess and properly deal with Mrs Dranty several months ago.

She appears.

"Why is this in our draft folder?" Gary points to the application.

Janet puts on her glasses and squints at the tiny writing.

"Oh, yes. I remember that. It's

the application for a Ukrainian refugee. I was wondering the other day why we haven't heard anything yet," Janet says.

"I know what it is! I mean, why is it here, in our drafts folder? That means it was never sent," Gary says, trying to remain calm.

"Oh, you know me and technology. But I definitely sent it," Janet breezes.

"You definitely didn't!" Gary exclaims. "Have you any idea what this is going to do to me if I'm elected??"

"What do you mean? Oh, because you've told them all that you're going to be receiving Ukrainians?" Janet suddenly twigs.

"Not only that, but some of the papers think we've already got some. I didn't bother to correct them as at least we'd applied. But now we haven't even done that. What a disaster!" Gary is dismayed.

"Why don't we just apply now?" Janet says, trying to helpful.

"That's not the point. It'll look as if I lied. I've already had to hide away for months to avoid our neighbours. Now, it'll be even worse."

Gary feels the weight of the world on his shoulders. He's also been attacked for attending services for all the different faiths. They're *all* offended as they say he isn't really committed to any of them and his attendance is a shallow gesture. The person who wrote the original article suggesting that aspiring councillors should attend multi faith meetings hadn't mentioned that this might be the outcome so Gary feels aggrieved. He was just trying to respect diversity.

The small church that hosts the drop in are also annoyed that Gary isn't attending *their* services. They saw in the media that he is now attending the much larger Parish church around the corner and don't understand why he doesn't join them on Sundays as he's already involved in their work.

Gary's campaign website is up and running but keeps getting hacked and he's had to close the message board due to spam and vicious messages being frequently posted including several that have threatened to kill him.

Gary is still rushing around helping with community projects but he's now attending far more meetings than anything else. He often finds that he has no idea how to even begin solving some of the problems that arise. Not finding a solution seems to anger people. The anger is often directed at him as the one who has failed to come up with a workable solution.

Gary is also living in fear that his son Dean's alcoholism and wild behaviour will taint him by association. To date, Dean hasn't done anything criminal, as far as he's aware, but his son has definitely reverted to teenage behaviour, is often drunk and is spending lavishly.

Grant too, now with no suitable

role model, has moved beyond his religious phase and is venturing down a dubious path. Although, Gary feels this might be better for his grandson, at least more in keeping with his age, than the Christian fanaticism he had been displaying before, he is concerned about negative publicity.

Although he won't admit it to anyone, Gary sometimes wishes he had never started the election campaign. He had been happier when he was just pootling around and helping his neighbours every so often. The campaign has taken on a life of its own and has taken over everything. Gary feels the pressure of other people's expectations. He knows it is also negatively affecting Janet who is often rushing around on his behalf.

Nevertheless, he can't bring himself to pull out when he is so close to victory. He still relishes the thought of the power that will come with the role. He longs to be well thought of and for people to see that he really is a good person. If he can just distance himself from those who've seen him mess up and know he's fallible, and if people would give him a chance, he will be a great councillor and everything will be all right in the end.

# Chapter 14

The election result is in! Gary will become Councillor Yale. It seems his lack of transparency regarding the hosting of a Ukrainian family hasn't affected his chances, nor his involvement in the various disasters of his neighbours, not his suspension on suspicion of assaulting a pupil all those years ago, and not even the wild behaviour of his relatives. Either people don't know, or they just don't care. The verdict is in and Gary is basically a good guy.

They celebrate with lobster and champagne at Gary's favourite restaurant. Gary decides not to dwell on the narrowness of his victory. A victory is a victory and he deserves some good fortune after all he has suffered.

They are just tucking in to their hearty meal when Janet points across the restaurant to a small table with a lone figure.

"It's Mr Fordy," she mouths.

Gary sighs. "Has he seen us?" he asks. "I forgot to talk to you about arranging a cleaner. His place was a real mess when I went there last time."

"Oh? When was that?" Janet asks, surprised. "I thought the last time you saw him was when Bertha had just died. I didn't think you'd even been to Bertha's funeral, did you?"

"No, I couldn't make it as something else came up," Gary lies and suddenly remembers that he hasn't told Janet that, going explicitly against her wishes, he had secured his final nomination from the *very* recently bereaved Mr Fordy. "I went round there another time to see how he was."

"He looks okay," Janet observes. "Oh, look. He's coming over.

"Congratulations Councillor Yale," Mr Fordy says as he arrives at their table. "And thankyou for the bench, it's a nice memorial. Remember you promised to do something about the speeding as well. Nice seeing you both." He hobbles out of the restaurant.

"Bench? Speeding thing? Memorial?" Janet says. She looks totally baffled.

"Yes. Just a few things he asked for if I became councillor," Gary waits for his wife to figure it out knowing she will. He braces himself for the tongue lashing.

Janet face changes to thunder. "I don't believe it. You actually asked for his nomination when he'd just lost Bertha. What is wrong with you?"

"It worked out okay and I will do something about the speeding when I get a chance," Gary says. "Look, it wasn't my fault Bertha died and Mr Fordy's never blamed me for not taking him to the hospital. I don't really think I did anything wrong."

"You never do," Janet mumbles and looks away. She's been forced on many occasions to intervene to protect her husband's reputation and she's fed up of him justifying himself.

Gary knows what she's thinking.

"I just try to help people and sometimes things go wrong, or people don't like the result, or they want more than I can give. Should I just not get involved and leave them to their own devices?"

"I don't know, dear. I just feel that I spend a lot of time defending you and trying to make sure people understand that your motivations are good. But watching the way you went about winning this campaign sometimes makes me wonder whether I know the real you at all," Janet says wearily.

"What do you mean?" Gary asks, he is on edge.

"Well, things like using our kindness to Sophie to show that you are a family man when really any grandparents would have done the same thing, and pretending that we hadn't been selected to host a refugee when we actually hadn't submitted the application, and a hundred and one other things like that. Is it really all worth it, all the pretence and using people, just to get to the top?" Janet feels that for herself it hasn't been worth it and she'd rather they could revert back to how they were before.

"I can explain all of those things and I did them for the right reasons. You'll see that none of them were really my fault and at least I'm not a criminal. You saw some of the things that came out above some of the other candidates. At least I try to do the right thing and I'm sure I've helped more people than not," Gary finishes.

Janet stares at her husband and they finish their meal in silence.

# Chapter 15

Councillor Yale sits on a park bench. He's feeling slightly woozy having just given blood but is proudly wearing the badge that announces that he is a "Super Donor". He feels good about his morning's work and is heading to a Council meeting in an hour or so. The sun is shining and the birds are twittering away. It's quite pleasant.

Now, he is rudely interrupted. He opens his eyes to find someone standing directly in front of him, blocking the sunlight that he had been enjoying. A youngish girl holding a piece of paper is hovering awkwardly.

"Hi, I'm sorry to disturb you. Would you like a Christian leaflet?" The girl asks cheerfully with a smile.

Gary remembers his new title and responds politely, as a councillor should,

"Well, I think perhaps you'd

better give that to someone else. I'm a Christian already. Thankyou, though."

"Oh, okay. Can I ask how long you've been a Christian for?" The girl looks genuinely interested and doesn't seem at all put out by his refusal of the leaflet.

Gary wasn't expecting the question, he hesitates,

"Well, all my life. This is a Christian country after all," he says.

"I became a Christian when I was 23," the girl responds.

"What were you before that?" Gary asks confused.

"A non-Christian or someone who didn't believe," the girl replies. "Can I ask you what you think the Christian faith is all about? I mean, what is the key message?"

Gary is starting to feel flustered by the questions and this over confident girl who seems to think he is deficient in some way. It's making him a little uncomfortable.

"Well, it's about loving your neighbour, going to church, praying and doing good to everyone. I'm a councillor, I go to church every week….and I was christened." Gary adds the last feeling that it won't hurt his case. He feels sure this girl will leave him alone now that he's proven himself, but she is staring down at him with what looks like pity!?

"It sounds like you do a lot of good. Do you think you will get to Heaven?" the girl asks.

"That's a bit deep isn't it? If there is such a place, yes I've done my bit," Gary answers confidently.

"But are you sure? I mean, how good do you have to be? How do you think God decides who He lets in?" the girl persists.

Gary is feeling irritated. Who is this girl to judge him, a well respected councillor, at least twice her age. "Yes, I'm sure, are *you* sure?"

"Yes, I'm sure," the girl matches Gary's confidence but he no longer feels confident. The girl is unsettling him.

"What have you done? I've helped people all my life, given to charity, driven mini buses for special needs kids, helped at a drop in and soup kitchen, wanted to host a Ukrainian refugee (he can't quite bring himself to lie to this girl), supported my family, and I'm a Super Donor." He points to his badge but even as he does this he feels a bit pathetic knowing he doesn't have to prove anything to this stranger in the park, but feeling inexplicably compelled to do so.

"It's not a competition. I was trying to show you that being a good person isn't what it's all about. God doesn't judge us based on whether we are good or not. If He did then we all fail and none of us would get to Heaven," the girl has sat on the bench and seems determined to continue this conversation.

At least she's out of his sun now. Gary looks at his watch. He doesn't need to be anywhere just yet. He might as well finish this. He feels sure he can beat this young girl at her own game.

"Didn't Jesus say that we should love God and love our neighbour. Those are the greatest commandments, right?" Gary asks.

"Well, yes, but we can't love God or our neighbour perfectly all of the time. That's the point. We aren't perfect and God's standard is perfection. He gave us the law to show us that we can't live up to it," the girl explains.

"Nonsense. What's the point in having rules if they can't be followed. That's not right, besides I follow the rules and compared to everyone else, I'm a good person. I'm sure of it. That's why I was elected to be a councillor because I'm a pillar of the community," Gary says proudly. As he says this, he is reminded of his underhand tactics in securing some of his nominations and of the various issues that have arisen due to his selfish motivations. He pushes this out of his mind. This girl doesn't know anything about him.

"Compared to God, none of us are good. The Bible says that if we say we haven't sinned we are saying that God is a liar and the truth isn't in us," the girl says softly. She looks at Gary intently.

"I'm not saying that I never do anything wrong, just that compared to others I'm pretty good and I'm sure the Man Upstairs, if he exists, will let me into Heaven, if there's such a place," Gary says, "In fact, I reckon they'll be over the moon to see me on that day!"

The girl winces and her expression changes. She stands up.

"I have to warn you that you're on the wrong path. I don't mean to be disrespectful as you clearly have more life experience than me. There are two types of people in Heaven, perfect which none of us are and forgiven. I've been forgiven by trusting that Jesus died for me on the cross and....."

Gary cuts across her, "I've heard

this nonsense before. I don't care to hear it again and certainly not from the likes of a young girl like you. I don't know who you think you are. I'm a respected councillor! How dare you tell me that I'm on the wrong path."

"I'm sorry for upsetting you, Sir. I hope that one day you'll understand why I tried to tell you the truth. I don't usually give this booklet to people as it contains a tough message, but I believe it is what God wants to say to you today." The girl places a small blue booklet next to him on the bench. She quickly walks away.

Gary huffs to himself about the audacity of the girl. He glances at the booklet realising that now that she's left it next to him he'll either have to take it with him, or find a bin. He can't just leave it there, or do what he really wants to do and tear it up and throw it back at the girl as someone will report him for littering. Besides, she's nowhere to be seen.

He's also curious about her last statement that the booklet contains a tough message. Gary is brave enough for anything and feels sure that nothing contained within a small booklet written by a religious zealot will phase him.

He picks the booklet up and reads the front cover.

*"The Parable of the Pharisee and the Tax Collector (Luke 18 vs 9-14)"*

Gary has never heard this story before so, intrigued, he turns the page and reads the following:

*"To some who were confident of their own righteousness and looked down on everyone else, Jesus told this parable:'Two men went up to the temple to pray, one a Pharisee and the other a tax collector. The Pharisee stood by himself and prayed:'God, I thank you that I am not like other people— robbers, evildoers, adulterers— or even like this tax collector. I fast twice a week and give a tenth of all I get.' But the tax collector stood at a distance. He would*

*not even look up to heaven, but beat his breast and said, 'God, have mercy on me, a sinner.' I tell you that this man, rather than the other, went home justified before God. For all those who exalt themselves will be humbled, and those who humble themselves will be exalted."*

# Note to Reader

Gary Yale appears to be an upstanding citizen. Since his retirement, he has been tirelessly helping others. However, he often acts without consideration for his wife and most of the time his motivations are selfish.

Gary wants to be popular, well-thought of and a pillar in the local community. He's happy to use people that cross his path in order to succeed. Over time, his conscience is dulled and he feels less and less guilty about his actions.

When Gary's corner cutting and lies catch up with him, he distances himself from the mess and blames others. He is self satisfied, looking down on and judging others, and thinking of himself as basically a good guy.

At the end of the story, Gary is confronted by a Christian who, not knowing anything about him, expresses some truths that he finds uncomfortable and therefore refuses to hear.

Many of us are just like Gary, we may not do things in the same way, or to the same extent, but we often have mixed, or wrong motivations for our good deeds. We may go through religious rituals, or claim to be obeying God, but who are we really serving?

The Bible tells us the truth; we cannot restore our broken relationship with God, or find peace with Him by doing good deeds. No matter how much good we do, it will never make up for the wrong we have done. Our goodness is always tainted by sin.

Gary refused to hear the answer to his sin problem. He didn't even accept that he had a problem preferring to justify himself. We aren't told whether Gary recognised himself in the parable at the end, but unless he is willing to humble himself and ask God for forgiveness, he will face an angry God on Judgement Day.

The parable of the *Pharisee and the Tax Collector* is an illustration Jesus used to highlight the offence of self righteousness to God. The Pharisee, rather than praying, is essentially talking to himself about how good he thinks he is, whilst the tax collector recognises his sin and humbles himself before a Holy God, pleading for mercy. God justifies and forgives the tax collector but not the Pharisee.

Those who are forgiven will go to Heaven, not on the basis of their good works, but because they have believed that Jesus died on the cross for them and have received his perfect life as a free gift. It is on this basis only that we can be made right with God and have a home in Heaven.

Will you humble yourself like the tax collector or stand on your pride and self righteousness like Gary and the Pharisee?

*Please feel free to contact the author at [natalie.vellacott@gmail.com](mailto:natalie.vellacott@gmail.com) and if you have enjoyed this book, the author is always grateful if you can spare the time to leave a review at Amazon and Goodreads. Thankyou!*

Printed in Great Britain
by Amazon